POLLIC
AND THE
DREADFUL
DRAGON

MIKE WATTS

With Words by
HEIDE GOODY AND IAIN GRANT

Fortress Dread

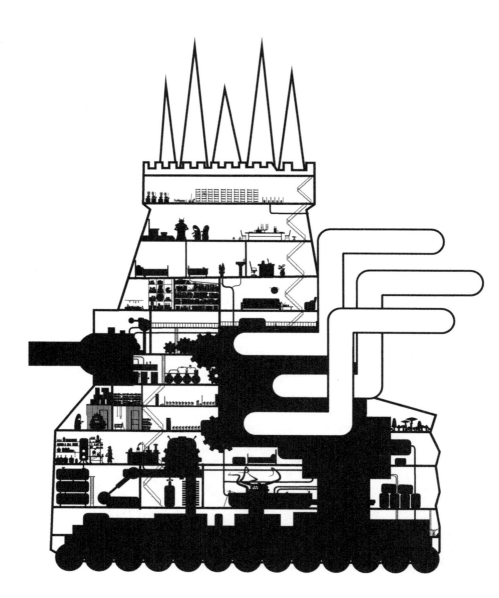

1

There was a natural order to things in Fortress Dread.

At the top was Lord Dread, obviously. Below him were his generals and advisors. He bossed them about and occasionally vaporised them with fireballs.

They, in turn, got to boss about their underlings: the battle chiefs, the evil sorcerers and the accountants. (Accountants are very important because you can't run an efficient evil Fortress if nobody gets paid.)

Below them were the gnomes.

Pollig the goblin felt that he should be allowed to boss the gnomes about because he was:

a) Bigger

b) Generally smarter and

c) Could play a tune using his armpit.

However, this was not the case. The gnomes got to boss Pollig about because they were all members of the Gnomish Workers Guild, which was apparently a big deal. Pollig was the lowest of the low and didn't get to boss anyone around, apart from the spiders. And even then only the little ones.

So when Dr Valeria Darkbottom – evil sorceress, general mixer of potions and all-round mad scientist – told Pollig to help her clear out and tidy up her Cupboard of Dangerous Chemicals, he didn't have the option to say no.

Pollig opened the door to the cupboard (which was more of a cavern) and looked at the horrible mess on the shelves and the floor. Broken bottles fizzed and bubbled. Multi-coloured clouds of horribleness writhed and fought each other. In the corner, pools of chemical goop had mixed and magically transformed a pile of rubber gloves into a flock of flying glove-birds.

Dr Darkbottom's heels clicked on the iron floor. Her snake familiar, Boomslang, flopped about her shoulders and sneered at Pollig. He shrank at the sight of Boomslang's mean little eyes.

Darkbottom grimaced at the mess in the cupboard. "When Lord Dread's Gravimatrix backfired, everything went sideways, goblin," she said.

Pollig remembered it well. The Dread Fortress had trundled across the country with the intention of blasting the city of Alderbaron into the sky with an anti-gravity ray. With their noble queen and shiny knights, their efficient sewers, and their free-to-use public libraries, the people of Alderbaron

clearly had it coming. It should have been a simple job, but there had been that annoying band of brave adventurers who had sneaked into the Fortress, switched around a couple of wires and, instead of Alderbaron shooting off into the clouds, Fortress Dread ended up with its own gravity swapped around. Left became down and up became right for a month.

"Going to the toilet was very difficult during that time," said Pollig.

"We don't want to know," said Boomslang. The snake was a very lazy creature who did nothing but flop about Darkbottom's shoulders like a slithery scarf and make sarcastic comments.

"Anyway, even though the Gravimatrix is safely turned off and locked away in Lord Dread's vault, we still have to clean up the mess left behind," said Dr Darkbottom. "Anything that's not broken, clean it and set aside. Bin anything that's broken. Sweep up the filth. Mop the mess."

Pollig didn't like the look of the hissing, fizzing gloop on the floor. Just putting a toe in that stuff might cause him to disintegrate, or be transmogrified into something horrid.

"This going to take a long time," he said.

"Got somewhere better to be?" sneered Boomslang.

"Actually, I was meant to be going to the supplies office to get some nose plugs for the gnomes on gunge cleaning duty. Those gunge pipes stink. By the way, don't I get any personal protection equipment?" he added.

"What?" snapped Darkbottom, who was already preparing to get on with other mad scientist business.

"A hazmat suit? Goggles?"

"Whatever for?" she asked.

"What if I tread in something and start to melt?"

Darkbottom fished around in the pocket of her lab coat and presented Pollig with a whistle.

"What's this for?" asked Pollig.

"If you start to melt, give three sharp toots on the whistle," said Darkbottom.

"And then what happens?"

"I'll know to send for another goblin."

Pollig looked at the whistle with mixed feelings.

"Say thank you," hissed Boomslang.

"Er, thanks," said Pollig and set to work.

He took a broom to the mess of smashed glass, bent equipment and spilled chemicals on the floor. When a pile of glowing crystals set the broom on fire, he carefully set it aside and tried mopping the floor instead. This worked well, until a leaky

potion turned the mop fibres into wriggling snakes. He tried to use the burning broom to kill the snake-mop, but the snakes wriggled with enjoyment as the flames lapped their scales, so he left them in a corner.

Old boxes made ideal stepping stones in the slime, enabling Pollig to reach the shelves. He collected the vials and tubs which hadn't been broken and, with his arms full, carried them outside to safety. He made several trips (during which only a few of the stepping stones dissolved or exploded and needed to be replaced). On his fifth journey he picked up a stout metal box with a welded-on lid. The box made a gurgling, snoring sound.

Pollig wasn't a fan of mysterious boxes that made weird sounds. He took it to Dr Darkbottom. "What's this, doctor?"

Darkbottom looked round from her work. "Oh, that. Definitely had an off-day when I made that. A Tuesday, I think."

Pollig put his ear to it and listened to the gurgling snoring. "What is it?"

"It's the day after Monday," hissed Boomslang.

"Take it to the incinerators," said Darkbottom. "It's highly explosive, but far too unstable to be of any use."

"It's dangerous?" said Pollig.

"Very," said Darkbottom.

"What if it explodes on the way to the incinerators?"

"Have you still got your whistle?"

"Yes," said Pollig.

"If you think it's about to explode, give three sharp toots."

"Thanks," said Pollig.

It was seven floors and a long walk from Dr Darkbottom's laboratory to the incinerators. A long walk through the winding tunnels and pipe-filled corridors of Fortress Dread.

Down here, one could always hear the muffled roar of the Fortress furnaces and the thrum of the engines which turned wheels as high as treetops.

On top of that, Pollig could hear a constant flippy-flappy sound.

"Bats?" he wondered and looked up. A small flock of rubber gloves had followed him from the lab.

"Go back," he said, waving a free hand at them. "You can't come with me."

He turned to continue and missed the first step on a flight of stairs. As he stumbled, the metal box flew from his hands and bounced – Thump! Bump! – down the stairs. Before he knew what he was thinking, Pollig was running down after it.

Thump! Bump! Bump! Thump!

He could hear that the gurgling snoring had stopped, and had been replaced by a loud and rising whine. As he reached the bottom step the box spun up into the air one final time. Pollig wished he hadn't been so quick to chase it.

He turned to run, but before he could take a single step the box hit the ground and...

Pollig sat up woozily. His brain was still rattling around inside his skull from the explosion. A flock of startled glove-birds circled his head. On the floor, where the metal box struck the ground for the final time, there was a great big smoking hole.

"Oh, biscuits!" said Pollig, seeing what he had done.

He crawled over on hands and knees to the edge of the hole. Metal shards of twisted flooring hissed as they cooled. He waved away the billowing clouds and looked down.

What was underneath this level? He couldn't remember. Fortress Dread was so many layers of rooms and machinery, he wasn't sure if anyone really knew what was in each level.

The hole was dark (as was often the case with holes) and Pollig could see nothing in its depths.

"Halloo!" he called. "Anyone hurt down there?"

His voice echoed, but there was no reply.

That, at least, was something, he thought. No one had been hurt by the explosion – which was a good thing. Unless, of course, they'd just been killed outright – which was not such a good thing. Pollig decided to be optimistic and assumed the best. Pollig liked being optimistic. It required less effort than actually worrying about things.

The little green hairs abruptly stood up on the back of his neck and a chill ran through him.

The Spooks had arrived.

"Ha-what do we have here?" said one.

"I tell you ha-what we have," said the other. "Ha-we have a suspicious circumstance."

The Spooks spoke softly and unhurriedly. This might sound nice but it wasn't. They were soft and unhurried in the way a massive snake swallows people whole and takes two months to digest them.

The Spooks lived in the cracks in the walls of Fortress Dread. Or possibly in the shadows. Or maybe under people's beds. Pollig didn't know and he didn't want to know.

What Pollig did know was that the Spooks appeared when you were least expecting it and asked questions. Very pointed and difficult questions. And if you didn't answer the questions correctly then you might be hauled away to the dank and horrible prison cells. If you were lucky. If you weren't, then the Spooks took you to wherever they went – the cracks, the shadows, whatever – and no one ever saw you again.

One Spook bent over and inspected the hole.

"Is this your hole, sir?" it asked.

"Er, mine?" said Pollig.

"Oh. It's a mine, is it?" said the other. "Ha-would you happen to have a mining licence?"

"N-no," said Pollig.

The Spook made a disappointed whistling noise, like it was sucking air through its teeth, except Pollig didn't know if Spooks had teeth or not.

"No mining licence? And no protective mining equipment either? A shocking lapse in health and safety."

Pollig was tempted to tell them he'd asked Dr Darkbottom for protective equipment and that she'd given him a whistle, but decided that probably wouldn't help.

"I mean, no, it's not a mine and it's not mine. It's a hole."

"It's a hole, he says," said one Spook.

"Ha-we can see that, sir," said the other, looming over Pollig. "There is definitely a hole where there shouldn't be one."

"This is an act of sabotage."

"Of vandalism!" agreed the other.

"Of downright naughtiness!"

"A hole where there shouldn't be one and by pure chance this little gnome is right next to it."

When Pollig looked round for a gnome but saw none, he realised they meant him. "I'm not a gnome," he said.

"It's not a mine and he's not a gnome!" said one of the Spooks. "Is nothing ha-what it appears to be?"

"I'm a goblin," said Pollig.

"Ha-what's one of them then?" said the Spook.

Pollig wanted to explain, but he was the only goblin in Fortress Dread. He'd never so much as seen another one. He sort of did a gesture with his hands and a bit of twirl to indicate himself.

"I am," he said. "I'm a goblin."

They bent over to inspect him. "Looks like a tall gnome to me," said one.

"A very tall gnome," said the other.

"Offensively tall!"

"Such long legs!"

"Ha-why are your legs so long?" said the Spook.

"If they weren't they wouldn't reach the floor," said Pollig.

The Spooks shook their heads disapprovingly. "So, if you didn't make this hole, who did?"

"Pardon?" said Pollig.

The Spook suddenly had a notepad and pencil in its hands. "Paddon, you say?"

"What?" said Pollig.

"Paddon Watt," said the Spook, writing it down slowly.

"Who is this Paddon Watt?" asked the other Spook.

"What?" said Pollig.

"Yes, Watt," said the Spook. "I take it you saw him do this?"

Pollig realised he was in one of those moments. Everyone experiences them. A crystal-clear choice. He could back-track, explain the misunderstanding and try to just get on with his day. Or he could do the easy thing and nod and agree and let the Spooks go away thinking that Paddon Watt was responsible.

Pollig did the easy thing.

He nodded. "Yep. That's right. Paddon

Watt. Ooh, he's a scoundrel, he is. Anyway, I've got be going—"

A Spook hand stopped Pollig as he tried to go. "Ha-we can't let you go without getting a description," said the Spook.

"A description?"

"Paddon Watt made this dangerous and illegal hole in the ground, sir. We will need a description."

"It's big and dark and goes down a long way."

"Not the hole, sir," said a Spook. "Paddon."

"Oh, him." Pollig scratched his chin thoughtfully. "Like a description of him? Height? Distinguishing features? Whether he wore a hat or not? That sort of thing?"

"Did he wear a hat?" asked the Spook.

"Er, yes."

"Ha-what kind of hat?"

"One with a, er, wide...?"

"Brim?"

"Exactly," said Pollig.

"And his face?" said the Spook.

"Oh, he had one of those," agreed Pollig. "Eyes. Nose."

"Ha-what sort of nose?" demanded the Spook.

"A normal sort of nose," said Pollig, touching his own.

"And hair?"

"A big moustache," said Pollig. "An evil moustache. And he had a gold tooth. And a bite out of one of his ears." He was starting to get into the swing of this lying business. The more he lied, the more the Spook wrote in its notepad.

"And he went off in, um, that direction," said Pollig, pointing at random.

"You have been very helpful, sir," said the Spook as they began to slowly fade into the walls.

"Anytime," said Pollig cheerily, glad to see them go.

One of them paused before disappearing entirely. It pointed up at the little flock of glove-birds. "Do you have a licence for those birds, sir?" it asked.

"They're not birds, they're gloves," said Pollig.

The Spook gave him a look that made Pollig shiver, then it was gone. He might have acted all cheery and confident in front of them, but the Spooks made his knees wobble with fear. Pollig looked down to check.

Yes, his knees were wobbling all right.

3

ollig was alone. He was alone with a great big hole. A great big deep dark hole.

Pollig's natural instinct was to just walk away but a great big deep dark hole was a dangerous thing. Anyone could just walk along and fall into it. It was true that anyone coming along this tunnel was likely to be a vile troll, wicked witch or a beef-witted cockalorum, and if they fell into a hole it was almost certainly no less than they deserved, but Pollig had a soft heart at times and felt even the vilest, wickedest

and most beef-witted individuals should be given some warning.

He found a grubby piece of charcoal by the wall and with it wrote on the tunnel floor.

"Problem fixed," he said, satisfied with himself, and went back up the stairs. The glove-birds began to follow him but Pollig shooed them away.

"Clear off! Go flap somewhere else. Make little glove-bird nests or whatever you want to do."

Once they were gone, he returned to Dr Darkbottom's laboratory. Darkbottom was mixing potions, combining something pink and frothy with something green and gloopy and making something grey that stank of sweaty feet. Pollig couldn't tell if that was what she had hoped to achieve.

"Ah, you made it back alive," she said.

"More's the pity," hissed Boomslang, unwinding from Darkbottom's shoulders just enough to fix Pollig with a nasty glare.

"Why wouldn't I make it back alive?" said Pollig.

"I thought Paddon Watt might have got you," said Darkbottom.

"What?" said Pollig.

"Exactly!" said Darkbottom and held up a poster. Beneath a heading that said, Wanted! For Unspeakable Crimes! was a picture.

"Biscuits! Those Spooks do work fast!" said Pollig.

"I was worried he'd got you while you were taking that box to the incinerator," said Darkbottom.

"You were worried about me?" said Pollig, touched by the unusual display of concern.

"I was concerned about the box falling into the hands of a criminal like Paddon Watt."

"No one cares about you," sniggered Boomslang. "Even your fleas talk about you behind your back."

"You did take the box to the incinerator, didn't

you?" said Darkbottom.

Pollig didn't have a great answer to that question, so he went with "Um."

Darkbottom drew herself up in haughty anger. "What happened, goblin?"

"There's now this hole in the tunnel near the incinerator..." he began.

Darkbottom gasped, clutching Booslang. The snake wriggled unhappily as Darkbottom's nails raked along her scales. "Don't tell me, he leapt out and snatched the box from you!"

"What?"

"Yes! Him! He did, didn't he?"

Pollig was once again faced with the option of telling the truth. It was an easier decision this time.

"That's exactly what happened," said Pollig.

"Paddon Watt leapt out of the hole, grabbed the box and ran away."

"And you did nothing?" hissed Boomslang. She was free of Darkbottom's fingernails now and rolled her mean little eyes at Pollig's stupidity.

"You could have raised the alarm," said Darkbottom. "Why didn't you blow the whistle I gave you?"

"I thought that was only for if I was melting or about to explode."

"Stupid goblin. You have no sense of initiative."

"I don't think I was given one," he said honestly.

Number One, the head gnome, entered the laboratory. Number One, despite his high rank, was a small gnome and always accompanied by Number Two to open heavy doors and shout at people who were likely to tread on him.

"Excuse us, comrade-doctor," he said to Darkbottom. "We were wondering if you'd seen— Ah!"

This "ah!" was for Pollig. It was an accusing "ah!" and likely to be followed by a vicious telling off.

"The gunge pipe cleansing department are still waiting on their nose-clips, Comrade Pollig!" said Number One sternly.

"Ah," said Pollig. This particular "ah" was more

of an "oh, no", but just as likely to be followed by a vicious telling off.

"Maybe Paddon Watt stole those as well," sneered Boomslang.

"Yes!" said Pollig. "He did."

"What?" said Number One.

"The very same," said Darkbottom and waved the wanted poster in front of the gnomes' faces.

Number One and Number Two inspected it with the most serious of expressions. Number Two tugged fretfully at the tip of his hat.

"Doesn't look like one of our lot, boss," he said.

"Should think not!" said Number One. "Our brothers and sisters of the Gnomish Workers Guild are honest and trustworthy." He tapped the poster. "What unspeakable crimes has this Paddon Watt committed then?"

"Can't say. They're unspeakable," said Darkbottom.

"True, true," said Number One with a sad shake of his head. "The very worst crimes. And now the gunge pipe crew will have to soldier on with their task with nothing to block the gungesome smells from their noses. Awful!"

"Terrible!" agreed Number Two.

"I could always go and get some more," suggested Pollig.

Number One pulled back in surprise. "You would do that?"

"Seems only sensible," said Pollig.

"You'd risk your life for your comrades?"

"Risk my life?"

"With this dastardly, thieving, murderlising subversive Paddon Watt on the loose."

"Murderlising?" said Number Two.

"I should think so."

"Oh, that," said Pollig. "Yeah, I think I'll be all right."

Number One gripped Pollig's knee in a gesture of thanks. He might have wanted to slap Pollig's shoulder or shake his hand, but the gnome simply wasn't tall enough.

"It's an honour to have comrades such as you in the guild," he said, eyes gleaming with pride.

"He's not in the guild," said Number Two. "He's a goblin."

"Shame, shame," said Number One. "But them's the rules," he added. "Would have been good to have you. The guild looks out for its members and fights for fairness and equality for all."

"As long as they're gnomes," said Pollig.

"Exactly," said Number One.

4

Pollig came to the gunge pipe crew later in the day with a box full of nose-clips. The stinking crew of little gnomes mobbed him to get their hands on the stench-blocking clips. They greeted him, not with boos and mocking for taking so long (which was probably what he deserved) but with cheers and comradely pats on his ankles or knees, or whatever bits they could reach for braving the dangerous tunnels and putting his life at risk for them (even though there had been no real risk at all).

Pollig enjoyed the thanks and the praise even though he didn't deserve it. He positively drank it in. "Thank you, thank you all!" he said. "Happy to help!"

Something clung to his knee. It was Pollig's best friend, Number Twelve, giving Pollig a rare hug.

"You are my hero, Comrade Pollig."

"Yeah, yeah. All right," said Pollig, embarrassed, and gently prised him away.

The gnomes of Fortress Dread gathered round Pollig wherever he went that day, keen to either give thanks to their 'brave comrade' or, more often, get the latest gossip regarding this new and dangerous outlaw, Paddon Watt.

In the gnome canteen that evening, all the gnomes sat down to eat. Pollig was squashed up at the far end, looming over the tiny table next to his friend, Twelve.

It had been green slops for starters and looked like it was going to be yellow slop for mains. Twelve hated yellow slop – absolutely detested it – so they always agreed to swap. Twelve had Pollig's portion of green slop and Pollig had Twelve's portion of yellow slop. While they waited for the yellow slop to turn up, gnome Number One banged on the table for attention. He was barely heard over the general chit-chat, or seen, come to that. Number Two bellowed for everyone to shut up and listen, which they did, once again demonstrating why the head gnome always made sure he had a big Number Two whenever possible.

"Comrade Pollig!" called Number One down the length of the table. "Why are you here when you have not finished your chores? There are spiders in the ventilation shaft near Lord Dread's treasure vault! It's your job to get rid of them!"

"Oh, biscuits," muttered Pollig who had clean forgotten to do it. It was a job he hated.

"Did Paddon Watt put them back after you herded them out?" asked a middle-number gnome somewhere further down the table.

This caused gasps of shock.

"He did?" said another.

"He did!" said a third.

"Is this true?" Twelve asked Pollig, eyes wide.

Pollig considered his options.

He shook a fist at the ceiling. "Curse you, Paddon Watt!" he cried. "How could you?!"

This 'news' of fresh crimes caused a worried stir among the gnomes, but at least Pollig got to enjoy his yellow slop main course without further tellings off.

Throughout the week, it became easier and easier to blame Paddon Watt for any mistakes Pollig made, or tasks he failed to do.

When Pollig's sluicing and mopping of the dungeons was judged to be sub-standard, Pollig pointed at the smears of dirt still on the floor and said, "It was sparkling clean when I finished the job. Do you think Paddon Watt came in here and made some more filthy marks?"

The gnomes inspected the evidence and gave worried shakes of their head before sending Pollig on his way.

When a glass vial was broken in Dr Darkbottom's laboratory, Pollig quickly turned his guilty expression into a shocked and innocent one.

"Did you see?" he said. "Paddon Watt came running through, knocked it over and leapt out, er, that window there."

Dr Darkbottom rushed to the window and

looked out. "I cannot see him."

"Master of disguise, isn't he?" said Pollig.

Boomslang glared at Pollig suspiciously.

When gnome Number One found Pollig next to a plate on which there had been a pink frosted donut only a minute before, Pollig immediately said, "Paddon Watt came in here and took your donut. That's clearly what happened."

Number one stared in horror at his empty plate. He then stared at Pollig.

"Why are there crumbs of pink icing around your mouth, comrade goblin?"

"I was licking the plate to find clues," said Pollig.

"And what did you find out?" said Number One.

"That Paddon Watt likes pink donuts. Tasty, aren't they?"

And even though Pollig found it easier and easier to lie about what he had or hadn't done, he was shocked by what he heard in the corridor the following day.

"Are you sure you oiled Nobboth's gears, comrade?" one gnome was asking.

"I did, comrade-overseer," the other replied.

"They sound very squeaky and Nobboth has been complaining."

The accused gnome mulled this over. "What I mean to say is that I did oil the gears but then that villain Paddon Watt appeared and poured grit over them."

"What?" said Pollig.

"Yes. Him. He poured grit on the gears, I tell you," said the gnome with a scowl for Pollig for daring to question him.

"You saw him?" said Pollig.

"With my own eyes," said the gnome.

Pollig couldn't say why, but he felt that lying about an entirely imaginary criminal in order to make his own life easier was one thing, but other individuals shouldn't be allowed to use his imaginary criminal to excuse their own laziness! How dare they! If they wanted to blame their mistakes on a made-up baddie then they should make up one of their own!

Angered, he stormed into the gnome barracks and to the little kitchen where he knew he'd find his buddy, Number Twelve, who was on tea-making duty for the workers.

"You'll never guess what's happened," grumbled Pollig as he set about making himself a mug of tea in his little chipped mug. "I've just seen—" He stopped and looked round. "Where's the sugar cubes?"

Pollig liked a sugar cube or two in his tea. Or more accurately, he liked sugar cubes and only had the tea to justify having the sugar.

Twelve made a bit of a pretend go at looking for the sugar and then shrugged. "I think Paddon Watt came in here and stole them," he said.

"What?"

Twelve nodded. "He came in, grabbed them and ran out. I definitely didn't eat them all."

That was it!

Pollig snatched up Twelve in both hands. "No! He didn't steal them!"

"He did," insisted Twelve. "He, um, came in and told me to give him all the sugar and biscuits and cake, and then he ran off."

"No, he didn't steal them at all!" shouted Pollig.

"You don't know that!" Twelve shouted back.

"Yes, I do, because I made him up!"

"What?"

"Paddon Watt is a figment of my imagination. The Spooks asked me a question and they didn't hear me right and now everyone thinks there's a criminal on the loose in Fortress Dread when he never ever existed at all!"

The door to the kitchen slammed open. Number One stood there, the sternest of looks on his face. Number Two stood next to him (because Number One was too small to do that kind of door slamming by himself).

"You, comrade goblin, are in big trouble!" Number One snarled. "Very big trouble indeed!"

5

Pollig might have been four (or possibly five) times the size of Number One but Pollig was frightened of him all the same. And it wasn't because the head gnome had a big Number Two at his side either. Pollig was still three (or possibly four) times the size of Number Two.

Pollig was frightened because Number One, as head of the gnomes' guild, had the ear of certain dark mages and evil overlords and could have Pollig hauled off to a nasty cell or a horrible dungeon in an instant.

Pollig had no idea what the punishment was for inventing a goblin bandit and then blaming everything on him but it couldn't be good.

"Listen, sir, I don't know what you've heard—" began Pollig, then realised he was still holding Number Twelve. Gently, he put the gnome down. "I can absolutely explain everything, sir."

"I doubt that very much. I've never seen such unprofessional work!" growled Number One.

"Me?" said Pollig. "Unprofessional?"

"Don't you remember your basic H.O.L.E.

training?"

"H.O.L.E.?"

"He's not even taken the course," said Number Two witheringly.

"Not even taken the course," said Number One in disgust. "H.O.L.E. Holes – Observation, Labelling and Excavation. Your basic course regarding all hole identification matters."

Pollig gave a deep frown. Frowning came easily to him since there seemed to be so much in life that he didn't understand. He was beginning to suspect that Number One's anger wasn't directly connected to the sugar-stealing, spider-herding, donut-eating, dungeon-dirtying and entirely fictitious Paddon Watt.

"Hole?" said Pollig.

"Don't try to deny it," said Number One. "The Spooks found you by an unauthorised hole in the lower tunnels."

"I didn't make it. It's not my hole," Pollig lied.

"We know that!" grumped Number One. "But you did leave a sign to warn people."

"I did!" agreed Pollig.

"'Hol! Dangur!'" read Number Two from a piece of paper in his hand.

"Yes!"

"Entirely unacceptable!" snapped Number One. "Hol? Dangur? Sub-standard work, comrade goblin. What use is a safety sign that bad? Someone could have fallen in this hole, and who'd be to blame then, eh? If you'd remembered your training, you would know—"

"He hasn't done the course," Number Two reminded him.

"Hasn't done the course!" Number One hissed unhappily. "Curses! Number Two, get our comrade signed up for the next course. In the meantime, you comrade goblin need to get back down there and sort out your signage. It needs to be clear, effective and in line with gnomish working guidelines!"

"In line with what?"

Number Two produced a heavy instruction manual. The front cover showed two gnomes cheerily working together beneath the title: Staying Safe with Safety Signs. He tossed it into Pollig's hands.

"Take Number Twelve there with you," said Number One. "I want a hole that's clearly labelled and will make sure that everyone steers clear of that area. Get to it! Pronto!"

"We'll need more paint," said Number Twelve as they hurried away down the corridor. "Lots of different colours."

Pollig consulted the Staying Safe with Safety Signs book. "I wonder what it says in here about colour."

He found a chapter that was called What Colour your Sign Should Be. "Here we are. It says 'signs should be created in monochrome'."

Twelve looked up at him. "What colour is monochrome?"

Pollig shook his head and shrugged. "I'm not sure."

"Oh, this is hard," complained Twelve. "What else is in the book?"

Pollig read out a few of the chapter headings. "We've got Risk Assessments for Safety Signs, Who must be Consulted when you create a Safety Sign and, ooh, this could be useful, Some Working Examples of Safety Signs."

"Go to that chapter! We can copy that!" said Twelve.

Pollig found the chapter. It showed neat, black and white signs with messages like this:

Uneven surface. Take care!

and

Wear eye protection when using these tools

"So we can just change the words and use these signs!" said Number Twelve.

Pollig nodded at the idea. It was a sound approach, except for one nagging detail. "If we change the words, then it's like we've just invented our own sign again. It's not really copying, is it?"

Twelve sagged with disappointment. "You're right. It's a stupid idea."

"Or—" said Pollig, thinking, "—maybe we just change one or two words for each one. I think that could work."

They stopped by the Fortress gnome stores, which were staffed by a miserable looking gnome behind a wooden hatch.

"We'd like some sign stuff," said Pollig. He flicked quickly through the manual. "What I meant to say is we'd like some laminated pearlescent dungahyde, quarto-trimmed with rounded safety corners."

The gnome fetched a bundle of sign boards from some shelving at the back of his cupboard and slapped them onto the counter.

"And some monochrome paint, please," said Pollig. Pollig used the words 'please' and 'thank you' sparingly. In Fortress Dread, the various monsters and sorcerers didn't look kindly on goblins with good manners. However, the occasional 'please' seemed to be very effective, as though people somehow thought saying 'please' required a huge effort and was therefore a most precious thing.

The miserable gnome at the hatch seemed quite indifferent. "Monochrome paint eh? Is that black or white you'd be after?"

"Monochrome," said Pollig.

"Oh, I see!" said the gnome. "Been a while since someone asked me for that! How about striped paint, you could try that one?"

"No, monochrome. It says in here." Pollig pointed at the book.

"Or maybe you'd like some elbow grease, or a bucket of steam, or a long weight," sneered the gnome.

"You keep long weights in the stores?" said Twelve.

"Oh, yes," said the gnome, stroking his chin.

"How long?"

"Ooh. The longest." There was a glint in the gnome's eye as though he was enjoying a joke, but if there was a joke to be enjoyed, Pollig was unaware of it.

"Can I have a long weight?" said Twelve.

"We don't need a long weight," said Pollig.

"I just want to see what one looks like," said Twelve.

"We've got a job to do," said Pollig. "We need monochrome paint, not long weights."

The gnome at the hatch dumped two heavy tins of paint on the counter. One was black. The other was white. "Monochrome is black and white, fools."

"So, grey then?" said Pollig.

The gnome shook his head in exasperation. "Are you the kind of idiots we're getting in the guild these days?"

"I'm not allowed in the guild," said Pollig.

"I can see why," the gnome muttered.

Pollig gathered up the paint and the signs. Twelve picked up some paintbrushes.

"We not going to have a look at the long weights?" said Twelve, disappointed.

"We'll come back later," said Pollig.

"They might have run out by then," argued Twelve.

"Oh, I'll always have a long weight in stock for you," said the gnome behind the counter. Again, he had that knowing and amused look in his eye, even though Pollig had no clue what he found so funny.

"You say that, but what if Paddon Watt comes by and robs you, eh?" said Twelve.

The gnome looked panicked. "I don't want no trouble! I've heard that he's properly vicious."

"Ooh, he's dangerous," Pollig agreed. "Kicks dirt in gnomes' faces."

"Really?"

"Yup. He went to the accounts department and snapped all their pencils."

"No!"

"It's true. I heard he swapped the labels on the salt and sugar jars in the canteen so everyone put salt in their tea."

"The fiend!"

"I know!"

"I saw him bite a gnome's face off and spit it out just because he was looking at him funny!" Twelve yelled, excited by the game.

Pollig and the gnome stared at Number Twelve in horror.

"Crumbs, Twelve!" said Pollig, shocked. "Where do you come up with stuff like that. Just imagine if some kids heard you say that. It's enough to give them nightmares."

"I'm closing the stores!" said the gnome in panic. "It's too dangerous!"

The gnome shooed them away and closed the shutters on the hatch. There was the click and clank of locks being locked and then the sound of furniture being piled up against it.

"Now I'll never get a long weight, will I?" grumped Twelve, angry with himself.

Pollig patted his friend affectionately. "Never say never. Hang around long enough and I'm sure you'll get one in the end."

6

Seven floors down and along a dank dark tunnel, they found the hole. Twelve whistled, impressed at its dark depths. His whistle came echoing back, warped and strange.

"How did this happen, then?" said Twelve. "Was it that Paddon Watt character?"

Pollig shook his head. "Do I need to remind you that Paddon Watt is made up? He's a figment of my imagination."

"Oh, yeah," said Twelve. "But I'm imagining him too, now. Is he a figment of my imagination as well then?"

"I think he's only one figment," said Pollig. "Maybe he hops from head to head."

"Ooh, he's a clever one that Paddon Watt," said Twelve.

They got to work with their paints and boards. They had a pot of black paint and a pot of white paint and so, since the book clearly said they should make monochrome signs, they took a dip in each pot with their brushes and applied the swirly result to the signs.

They copied the signs from the book and changed the words just enough to suit the situation.

Wear Eye Protection When Using These Tools became: *Wear a Parachute When Falling Down Hole. Uneven Surface. Take Care!* became: *Invisible Surface. Death Will Surely Follow if you Tread On It!*

"These are dead good," said Pollig

They were pleased by their efforts, so they took some of the other examples in the book and came up with more signs. Eventually the paint ran out.

Pollig and Twelve stepped back to look at their achievement.

"Job done!" said Twelve.

"No one can say we didn't warn them about the hole now," agreed Pollig.

7

On Tuesday afternoons, Pollig and Twelve would meet in the fungus forest on the sixth floor of Fortress Dread in order to collect stinkfrond toadstools for the kitchens.

No one in the Fortress was sure if the fungus forest had been deliberately cultivated under Lord Dread's orders, or if the forest had sprung up naturally in the vast, damp and lightless space at the rear of the roving Fortress. It was a point of

much debate and discussion. Some argued that a fungus forest filled with fly-repelling wimbo mushrooms, pain-numbing giddy slime, and the surprisingly edible stinkfronds must have been created on purpose. Others pointed out that no sane being would have designed a fungus farm where one could be squashed by toppling splathorns, poisoned by spotted gillbotts, or enveloped in sticky spores by the trembling puffblowers.

It was a constant source of disagreement, but all Pollig knew was that a Tuesday afternoon of tiptoeing through the poisonous and carnivorous fungi (under the pale blue light cast by the massive onglelamp mushrooms) was dangerous, yet essential.

Today, however, his thoughts turned to the question of where Number Twelve might be. Pollig had been waiting around for a full hour with his mushroom basket. Twelve could not tell the time, nor could he wear a watch (even the smallest was too heavy for the tiny gnome), but it was not like him to be late.

"Where on earth can he be?" he asked a trembling puffblower.

He did not expect an answer. The bloated, air-filled fungus sack wobbled threateningly but that told him nothing.

"Here he is!" declared Number One loudly, striding towards Pollig through the fungus forest, as his Number Two swatted aside fungi that got in their way.

"Where?" said Pollig, looking around for Twelve and seeing no sign of him.

"Here!" said Number One, who was quite clearly annoyed. "The worst underling I've ever known."

"Twelve?" said Pollig.

"No! You!" scowled Number One. "I can't think of a more incompetent inhabitant of this Fortress, can you?"

"What?" said Pollig.

"Well, apart from Paddon Watt, obviously," said

Number One.

"Obviously," agreed Number Two. "Ooh, he's a rascal."

"Wouldn't be surprised if he tried to steal all of Lord Dread's gold or something."

"Wouldn't be surprised at all, comrade-sir."

"But what have I done?" asked Pollig. "Or is it something I haven't done?"

"Oh, it is definitely something you have done, comrade goblin!" said Number One.

"It would have been better if you had done nothing at all," said Number Two.

"You were given clear instructions," said Number One. "Clearly label that hole, I said."

"I did!" said Pollig. "We did! Number Twelve and me! He'll tell you."

"Don't bring Comrade Twelve into this. Besides he's on an important errand for me right now."

"He's been sent for one of those extraordinarily long weights for which the supply stores are famous," said Number Two. "He couldn't stop talking about it, so we decided to order one just to see how long they are."

"He's been gone quite a time now," said Number One.

"Oh, I'm sure our patience will be rewarded, comrade-sir."

Number One refocused his anger on Pollig. "We told you to put signs up around the hole and make sure that everyone steers clear of that area!"

"We did," said Pollig.

"Oh? Then how come every gnome, troll, orc and cockalorum in the Fortress seems to be down there right now."

"What?"

"Yes, Paddon Watt too, probably. Your signs have made the hole positively alluring. Everyone's gone to have a look. You've turned it into a blooming tourist attraction, comrade! You tell people there's a deep hole, they'll want to know how deep. You say something is dangerous, they'll want to see the danger."

"So, you told me to put signs up around the hole because it was dangerous, and now people know it's dangerous, they're going to have a look to see just how dangerous it is?"

"Exactly!"

"Well, if you don't mind me saying, those people are just stupid."

"Of course they are," said Number One. "Doesn't mean this isn't your fault, though. People have been stupid since the dawn of time. You should have taken that into account when choosing your signage."

Pollig picked a stinkfrond and put it in his basket. "I'm not sure what you want me to do about it."

"Fix it, comrade goblin! Fix it!"

Pollig had no idea how to do that, but the chief gnome had a determined look on his face and when he gave an order, Pollig had no choice but to obey. With his basket over his arm (with just one stinkfrond mushroom in it), Pollig headed out of the fungus forest. Near the exit, he kicked a trembling puffblower in frustration. It exploded, sending out sticky spores. Pollig hurried on before any of them could reach him.

He hastened down the many staircases, ramps, secret chutes and dark passageways that led to the tunnel and the hole.

A great crowd of Fortress citizens were gathered round the hole. Flashes popped and smoked as dark wizards snapped pictures with magic camera contraptions. Visitors stood as close as they dared to the edge and shouted into the black abyss. An enterprising troll was selling postcards of the hole. Another was doing improbably brisk trade selling pebbles marked with the words: My friend visited the hole but all I got was this lousy pebble.

An energetic gnome waved a yellow umbrella in the air and led a party of visitors around the edges of the hole.

"And from this angle we can clearly see that the hole goes down many, many metres," he lectured to his band of tourists. "Legend says that if you stare too deeply into the hole, evil spirits will come to your home and steal your shoes."

"What legend?" demanded Pollig.

"The legend of the Deep Dark Hole," said the gnome without hesitation.

"How can there be a legend? This hole is nearly brand new!"

"All legends have to start at some point," replied the gnome. "This just happens to be a quite new legend. Anyway, what do you know?"

"I know that this hole is very dangerous and you should all get well away from it," Pollig said loudly so that everyone could hear.

"Oooh," said many of the onlookers, keen to hear juicy details.

"How do you know that?" asked the tour guide gnome.

"Because I was here when the explosion made the hole. You should leave because we have no idea what damage it may have caused!"

"Ooooooooooh!" The people pressed in closer, eager for more.

"This whole area could be unsafe!" Pollig yelled. "The rest of the floor might vanish underneath us at any moment! You should run!"

The tourists were fascinated.

"Which bit of floor?" asked an evil witch. "This bit of floor? Quick! Rhinophyma! Take a photo of me while I stand on the dangerous bit!"

With every dire threat Pollig uttered, the denizens of Fortress Dread only became more interested. The more he tried to drive them away with warnings, the closer they gathered about him.

"Crumbly biscuits!" he yelled in fury. "You're all IDIOTS!!"

"Oo you callin' an idiot?" demanded a cockalorum.

"You!" snapped Pollig. "You're all idiots because—" He looked at the circle of unhappy and insulted creatures, nearly all of whom were many, many times his size. "Because—" He thought fast. Pollig did not consider himself to be a clever goblin but he had a keen desire to survive the day so he made his brain work overtime. "Because – if you think this hole is dangerous then you clearly haven't seen the rickety staircase on level twenty-one."

"Eh?" said the cockalorum.

"The staircase on level twenty-one, near the flarb capacitors," said Pollig. "Some of those handrails have rusted right through. You touch them and you'll cut yourself, catch a deadly disease and fall down the stairwell to your death all in ten seconds flat."

"S'true," said a gnome. "Right shoddy workmanship on them stairs."

"That's way more dangerous than this hole," said Pollig.

Some of the creatures began to shuffle off.

"But! But!" Pollig called after them. "If you're looking for real danger then you should see the loose door on the furnace on level nine."

"Really?" said a fascinated troll.

"I'm not saying you should go anywhere near it," Pollig warned them, "but I reckon if you even touched it might just fall off and you'd be immediately burned to a crisp by a great big blast of fire. Wallop. Sizzle. Dead."

The crowd of tourists ran for the stairs to the upper levels. He didn't know if they were going to pay a visit to the rickety stairs or the faulty furnace. He didn't care. They were leaving, which was very much the point.

A dark wizard gave Pollig a snooty look as he packed away his camera tripod.

"Actually, most accidents happen in the home," he sneered. "Eleven thousand people are injured each year by socks, you know."

"Good job I don't wear any then," said Pollig, waggling his toes.

As the dark wizard strode off in his curly-toed shoes, Pollig found himself to be alone by the hole, apart from the two entrepreneur trolls. The souvenir-pebble seller threw down one of her pebbles and tutted.

"Thanks a bunch, goblin!" she grumbled. "I've got two hundred souvenir pebbles now and no one to buy them."

"It took me ages to make these postcards," said the other one.

The postcard was a ragged white rectangle of card with a black splodge in the middle.

"Gonna have to make me a load of wobbly stair postcards now," she grunted and gave Pollig a moody shove.

Pollig stumbled back. His heels touched the edge of the hole. His arms whirled as he tried to stop himself tipping over. He had no idea if the arm whirling had any effect (apart from startling the glove-birds overhead). He teetered, he wobbled and then managed to throw himself forward and safely onto firm ground.

The trolls were stomping off.

"Stifling local business start-ups, you is," said one troll.

"No respect for the small business owner," said the other.

And then they were gone.

Pollig looked about. Yes, he had successfully driven them all away with mostly made up stories of more dangerous tourist attractions elsewhere.

"Well done, Pollig," he told himself.

He turned and stepped on the discarded souvenir pebble. The pebble and his foot slid on the floor. Pollig's legs went from under him, he did an unintended backflip and fell right down the hole.

8

Pollig fell for what felt like a long time. He fell, then he slid, then he scraped and bounced and rolled. Then he fell some more. He spun, he whirled (he was sure he did a little loop-the-loop somewhere) and finally came to a stop in complete and utter darkness.

In the darkness, he patted himself down to check that nothing was broken. His knee made a worryingly rattling sound, then he realised it was resting on the souvenir pebble which had fallen down with him. He seemed remarkably unhurt, which was a stroke of good luck.

Obviously, he was remarkably unhurt and stuck at the bottom of a deep dark hole, so deep and so dark that he couldn't see his hand in front of his face. He probably wouldn't be able to climb out again. So, overall, luck was not necessarily on his side.

He put out a hand and felt for a wall. It was curved and damp. He tapped his feet. The floor was curved and damp too.

"Is this a pipe?" he said to no one at all. His

voice echoed faintly back to him.

"HELLO!" he yelled.

"HELLO! Hello! Hello-hello-'ello," came the echo.

Pollig listened to it fade away and, as it faded, he heard another noise. It was a gurgling, snoring sound. It sounded like water bubbling down a drain. It was a curious noise and he was sure he had heard it before, but could not remember where.

In the dark, he made his way towards the noise. He walked straight into something big and hard and fell down on his backside.

The gurgling snoring sound stopped at once. High above, two glowing eyes stared. They regarded him with snooty contempt.

"Who dares wander into the lair of Felfius Hypotenuse?" asked a very displeased (if slightly nasal) voice.

"I didn't dare do anything," said Pollig. "I just sort of walked into your ... your..." He waved in the dark at whatever it was. Was it a leg? A trunk? He didn't know. "What was your name?"

"Hypotenuse."

"Hypotenuse?"

"Hypotenuse," said Hypotenuse.

"High-pot-a-news. That's an odd name."

The creature gave a gurgling grumble. "You think it's funny? Are you poking fun at me? I'm the Queen of the Dragons, don't you know?"

"D-dragon?" said Pollig. His mouth fell open in surprise. In the dark, no one could see, but it fell open nonetheless.

"Of course, dingbat!" said Hypotenuse. "You

never seen a dragon before?"

Pollig wanted to say something, but his brain was paralysed with fear. Biscuits! A dragon in Fortress Dread? An actual fire-breathing dragon! And he'd run into its leg? As hard as iron, as immovable as a tree! And how high up were those eyes! It must be even bigger than Nobboth!

"Crumbly biscuits," he whispered in fear. "Um, no. No, I've not seen a dragon before." In fact, he still hadn't seen one, apart from the glowing eyes, but he decided that, despite a tiny nugget of curiosity inside him, he would much rather be a living breathing goblin who had never seen a dragon, than a flame-crisped goblin who had.

"Well, I have taken up enough of your time," he said, slowly backing away.

"You must give me treasure before you go," said Hypotenuse.

"What treasure?"

"Treasure to add to my hoard, dingbat," she said.

"I don't have any treasure," he said.

"Everyone has something."

"Not me. I've got nothing but the clothes I'm standing in."

"Then they'll have to do, won't they?" she said, sniffily.

"My ... my clothes?" As he said it, he just knew that this massive scaly beast was making him take his clothes off so she wouldn't get stringy cotton fibres in her teeth when she ate him.

He took a stumbling step back and his foot connected with something. It was the souvenir pebble. Thinking quickly (but possibly not thinking things through properly), he grabbed it and hurled it at her evil eyes.

"Have this instead!" he yelled and prepared to run.

The pebble struck. There was a yip of painful surprise and a massive FOOM!

The pipe-like tunnel was suddenly awash with flame and Pollig could see clearly.

Atop a rusty old pipe there stood the smallest dragon that Pollig had ever seen.

(It was, of course, also the largest dragon he had ever seen, since he had never seen one before, but he was prepared to bet that if he ever saw another dragon it would have to be bigger than this one.)

"You hit me!" she squealed.

"I know who you are!" he shouted back.

"Right on the nose!"

"I thought I recognised that sound!"

"Enough to make my eyes water."

"You were in that box Dr Darkbottom gave me!"

"I'm going to get a bruise!"

"You caused the explosion that made the hole."

"I only breathe fire when I'm startled."

"You nearly burned my eyebrows off."

"You dropped me down the stairs!"

"You said you were the Queen of the Dragons!" said Pollig, now very much more angry than afraid. If he had time to think about it, he might have realised that he was angry with the little dragon for scaring him, but he was much angrier with himself for being so easily frightened.

"I AM the Queen of the Dragons!" she shouted.

"And where's your hoard of treasure?" he said because there was clearly none.

"I've just moved in. I'm getting started." She looked down at the pebble on the floor. "This is just the beginning. I'm sure the other treasure will be along in a minute."

"How?" said Pollig.

Hypotenuse jumped down from her high spot and moved the pebble around a bit with her snout until it was placed as she wished. "You have to speculate to accumulate," she said.

"What does that mean?" said Pollig.

"You have to have wealth to make wealth."

"Do you?"

"Obviously, you flip-flop!" she snorted. "That's why rich kings get even richer. I put this bit of treasure here—"

"I'm not really sure that's treasure," said Pollig.

"—and before you know it, some gold coins will turn up."

"Will they?"

"Stands to reason. It's called interest," said Hypotenuse. "The gold gets interested and comes along to see what's happening. And that adds to the pile so the pile creates even more interest and more treasure turns up."

"That doesn't sound quite right."

"Course it does. And who would know better? Me, a treasure-hoarding dragon or you—? What are you, anyway?"

"I'm a goblin," said Pollig.

"Oh," said Hypotenuse, clearly not interested. "Anyway, all you need is a bit of treasure and that attracts other treasure. It's like them wotsits that clump together."

"Wotsits?"

"White things."

"Sheep?" suggested Pollig.

"No. I mean those white fluffy things. Famous for sticking together in a big mass."

"Definitely sounds like sheep."

"No," said Hypotenuse hotly (and indeed a flicker of fame appeared briefly in one nostril). "You cook it up and eat it."

"Still sheep."

"And when it comes out of the pan all wet and claggy, it sticks together. That's how treasure works. S'basic magnetism."

"I don't think that's how you build up a treasure hoard at all," said Pollig.

"So what do you think happens?" sneered the

tiny dragon.

"I think you actually have to go and look for more treasure."

"What? Like with my eyes?"

Pollig nodded. "Think so," he said and then added, "I could help you look while I try to find my way out of here."

Hypotenuse gave him a suspicious look. "You think you're qualified to be my Assistant Treasure Hunter?"

"I think I'm heading out that way," said Pollig, pointing along the tunnel. "You're welcome to come with me. Any treasure we find you can have." He stuck a stick in a burning pile of rags and lifted it up to use as a torch. "This way then."

Hypotenuse followed him. "Do you have any skills, then?" she asked.

"What do you mean?" asked Pollig.

"To help find treasure."

Pollig shook his head.

"I was gonna leave this place anyway," she said, hurrying to keep up with him.

"Why?"

"I think there might be spiders."

"Are you frightened of spiders?"

She scoffed. "A dragon frightened of spiders? Don't be a ridiculous, dingbat."

They walked on a way through the damp, spooky tunnel.

"I can play tunes with my armpit," said Pollig eventually.

"Huh?" said Hypotenuse.

"You asked if I have any skills?"

"Will it help us find treasure?"

"No," said Pollig. "No. But it might scare spiders away."

They walked on a moment.

"It's worth a try," said the dragon.

9

P ollig had lived in Fortress Dread for years and years but even he did not know every chamber and passage of the massive rolling Fortress. The place was massive. No, more than that, it was MASSIVE!

Pollig had heard that Fortress Dread was so big that there was a team of gnomes in charge of replacing the Fortress's light bulbs one by one, and by the time they had done the entire Fortress, even the youngest members of the team had grown old and grey, and a new team of young gnomes had to be brought in to do the next lot.

So it was not surprising that, as Pollig and the tiny dragon Hypotenuse wandered the pipes and tunnels of Fortress Dread, Pollig had no real clue where they were going. They climbed, they slid, they wriggled, they trekked. They climbed rickety stairs and rusty ladders. They went through creaking doors that hadn't been opened in hundreds of years. They tried other doors that were locked or jammed shut or had horrible snarling things on the other side.

All the while, as they travelled together, Hypotenuse would point her little snout at some random thing nearby and ask, "Is that treasure?" And Pollig would reply, "No, it's not."

"Is that treasure?"

"No, that's a bucket."

"Is that treasure?"

"No, it's a bat."

"Is that treasure?"

"No, it's a glove-bird nest."

"What's a glove-bird?" Hypotenuse asked.

"Don't ask," Pollig replied.

Pollig was beginning to wonder if they would ever find their way out when he heard a curious noise from up ahead. It was a voice, a loud voice. It was a calm and yet urgent voice. He hurried forward.

An opening in the tunnel ahead led onto a narrow balcony which overlooked one of the great halls of Fortress Dread. Huge numbers of Fortress residents were busy below as searchlights swung across the scene.

"Be alert," came a giant, ominous voice from speakers above. "Paddon Watt, public enemy number one, could be anywhere. Is he in your home? Is he in your place of work? Is he standing next to you right now?"

Pollig and Hypotenuse looked at each other.

"Be alert. Be vigilant. Protect Fortress Dread," said the booming voice.

Down below, a regiment of hulking great orcs marched in unison, their spikey armour and even

spikier weapons clanking and scraping as they moved.

Trolls had set up a checkpoint near one of the entrances. There was a barbed-wire fence and barrier that went up and down. They questioned and checked everyone going in and out before lifting the barrier to let them through. Everyone seemed to be politely ignoring the fact that most of the people going in and out were gnomes who were short enough to walk under the barrier without it being lifted at all.

Cockalorums and evil wizard's apprentices were handing out Wanted! posters to every passer-by until everyone seemed to be carrying at least three. Up above, ginormous posters with Paddon Watt's face on it hung over the scene, wafting in the breeze from the Fortress's ventilation shafts.

Teams of dark sorcerers were practising their fireball spells. Alchemists were preparing vials of smoking liquid and melting holes in the floor and each other.

"Do not underestimate our enemy," said the booming voice. "He's stolen nose-clips. He's stolen donuts. He's stolen all of the long weights from the supply store. He sets off explosions and makes up dangerous rumours about wobbly stairs and broken furnace doors. He once bit a gnome's face off! Shocking!"

Pollig put his head in hands.

"This all looks very exciting," said Hypotenuse. "Are they going to war?"

"With an enemy that doesn't exist," Pollig groaned.

"Are you sure?" the small dragon said. "It looks like they've captured someone."

Pollig looked down. On the floor below, two Spooks slid along on whatever they had instead of legs, with a prisoner between them. The Spooks moved unhurriedly. Spooks were like the night. It didn't matter how fast you moved, the night would catch up with you anyway.

The prisoner held firmly between them was Number Twelve!

"I'm innocent!" yelled the unhappy gnome. "I didn't do nothing!"

"Didn't do nothing?" said one of the Spooks. "If you did not do nothing then you must have done something."

"You know what I mean!" wailed Twelve.

"We will soon find out ha-what you know and

don't know, sir," said the Spook. "You seem to know a lot about this Paddon Watt."

"You ha-were the last one to see the long weights at the store," said the other Spook. "And now there are none."

"You seem to know a lot about the hole ha-which he made."

"And no one else appears to have ha-witnessed the face-biting incident," said one Spook.

"Terrible business," said the other. "And now we ha-want to know about his plans to steal Lord Dread's gold."

"But I know nothing!" Twelve sobbed.

"Don't ha-worry, sir," said the Spook, carrying Twelve towards a secure door. "We have ha-ways of jogging your memory. Soon all manner of secrets will pour from your mouth."

"That's the most secure area of Fortress back there," said Pollig grimly. "Nothing but prison cells, dungeons and Lord Dread's treasure vault."

The big secure door closed after the Spooks and Twelve with a grim KA-CHUNK.

"Crumbly biscuits with cheese on top!" swore Pollig. "This is all my fault!"

"Is it?" said Hypotenuse, who was clearly impressed.

"If I hadn't dropped your box then there wouldn't have been that hole in the floor. And if I hadn't lied to the Spooks about Paddon Watt then there wouldn't be all this nonsense going on. And if I hadn't blamed Paddon Watt for all the things I did wrong or forgot to do then Twelve wouldn't have joined in and opened his big mouth and he wouldn't have been arrested by the Spooks and taken off to one of their horrible dungeons."

Hypotenuse was nodding her snout. "Gosh," she said. "Yes, that does sound like it's all your fault. You're a right flip-flop, aren't you?"

Pollig shook his head with deep sorrow and burning regret.

Down below, orcs marched and trolls bullied gnomes, and various sorcerers and mages prepared to unleash all manner of terrible spells on an unseen enemy.

"I've got to put this right before anyone gets hurt," said Pollig.

A wizard's practice fireball flew off course and accidentally blasted a troll twenty feet into the air.

"...Before anyone else gets hurt. Come with me, Hypotenuse, I might need your help." Pollig marched purposefully along the tunnel in search of a way down to the hall below.

"Wait!" shouted Hypotenuse excitedly. "I've got it!"

Pollig turned. "What is it?"

"Rice!" she said.

"Pardon?" said Pollig.

"The white stuff that sticks together when you've cooked it. Rice! That's what it's called."

Pollig blinked at her. "Come on, you daft dragon. We've got no time to lose!"

10

"Obviously." Pollig tried to act as if he knew exactly how he was going to do that. He peered at the puffblower's stalk. It was as thick as his arm. "I'll just cut it down then," he said.

He pulled out his tiny folding mushroom knife and sawed lightly at the stalk. Each motion of the blade made the puffblower wobble. He held the stalk with one hand while he sawed it slightly harder with the other one. It dipped and swayed much more violently than he would have liked.

"Pollig," said Hypotenuse.

"Yes?"

"I thought it was really important to keep it still?"

"Yes," he grunted. "Trying." He was about halfway through the stalk, and there was a low creaking sound. The stalk bent and snapped. Pollig dived to catch the upper part of the stalk and clasped it to his chest, his eyes screwed shut.

He opened his eyes to look at the puffblower's sack. It was just clear of the floor.

"Phew!" said Hypotenuse, trotting over. "I thought you'd dropped it."

Pollig got to his feet, very, very carefully, holding the puffblower at arm's length.

"We can go and find Twelve now!" he said proudly. He had another thought. "I might get a handful of stinkfronds as well. They might be useful."

"What are stinkfronds for?" asked Hypotenuse.

"Well, we eat them," said Pollig. "They lose their smell when they're cooked. But when they are raw, they smell really bad if you crush them."

He grabbed a small handful and crushed it to demonstrate.

"Oof!" Hypotenuse wrinkled her tiny snout. "Smells like an orc's underwear drawer!"

"Exactly," said Pollig and then felt compelled to ask, "How do you know what an orc's underwear drawer smells like?"

Hypotenuse held up her snout disdainfully. "I don't want to talk about. Let's just say, even the Queen of Dragons has to make her nest in unsavoury places."

11

P ollig and Hypotenuse walked down to the hall where they had last seen Twelve.

"So, let me get this straight," said Pollig. "You lived in an orc's underwear drawer?"

"I was hatched in one, I think," said the little dragon. "It wasn't a great introduction to life."

"And how long did you live there?"

"Until the first time I saw a spider," she said. "I was terrified and so..."

"Foom?" suggested Pollig.

"Foom," said the dragon sadly. "You know what smells worse than an orc's underwear drawer?"

"An orc's underwear drawer on fire?"

"Exactly."

Pollig and Hypotenuse reached the hall they had viewed from the balcony. A troll at a barrier checkpoint blocked their way.

The guard pointed to a nearby sign. "Can't you read? It says that you must present your papers at the barrier."

Pollig looked at the sign and frowned. "That can't be right."

"What did you say to me?" The guard towered over Pollig.

"Your sign. It's not right." Pollig rummaged around for the Staying Safe With Safety Signs book. He didn't have to rummage far as the book was so big. He flicked through the pages and held it up. "Look. Signs are supposed to be painted in monochrome, and yours is red."

"But that just means it's really important!"

"It's an incorrect sign is what it is," said Pollig puffing out his chest. "Ooh, somebody's in trouble."

"Big trouble," said Hypotenuse, happy to join in.

"I'd better go report this to the authorities," said Pollig with as much threat as a young goblin could muster.

"Authorities!" echoed Hypotenuse.

"What?" said the troll, starting to sound a little panicked.

"I shall go speak to the Spooks," said Pollig.

"Please don't!" said the troll, suddenly all

apologetic. "I didn't know it was wrong!"

Pollig tutted. "Sadly, ignorance is no excuse."

"I can fix it!" the troll wailed.

Pollig looked around, pretending to check no one was listening, and then whispered to the troll. "You fix the sign and I'll keep the Spooks busy and make sure they don't spot it."

"Oh thank you!" gushed the troll.

"Pop down to the gnome supply stores. They've got all the monochrome paint you need."

"Thank you! Thank you!"

The troll hurried off and Pollig and Hypotenuse trotted across the hall.

"This putting the wind up people and bossing them about business is fun," said Hypotenuse.

"Don't let it go to your head," said Pollig. "We're just doing it to get to Twelve."

"Of course." Hypotenuse strutted with her tiny nose held high. "You!" she snapped at a nearby wizard. "Tie your bootlace and straighten that robe!"

The wizard in question was so surprised he did

exactly as he was told.

There was such a state of panic that nobody stopped to ask why there was a tiny dragon walking amongst them. Searchlights scoured every corner of the vast space. The many minions of Lord Dread scrutinised each other, checking to see if Paddon Watt was hiding among them. The armies of Lord Dread prepared to do battle.

Pollig had to take great care of the puffblower as people rushed back and forth. Why did nobody look where they were going? He twisted and dodged to stop it from getting bashed.

They made it to the great big door through which Twelve had been taken. Pollig peered through the keyhole. "I think this door can only be opened from the inside."

"So, how are we getting in?" asked Hypotenuse.

Pollig looked at the large keyhole. He looked at the tiny dragon. He looked at the large keyhole again.

"Do you think you can fit through there?" he said.

"Why would I want to fit through there?" she replied.

Pollig scooped her up (making sure he didn't drop the fragile puffblower) and pushed her through the keyhole.

"This is very tight," grumbled the dragon and then immediately fell through the other side with a soft plop.

"Right," said Pollig. "You need to find a lever or handle or something to let me in."

"Lever ... handle..."

"Are you looking?" Pollig called through the keyhole.

"Of course I'm looking. Ah!"

"You found it?"

"Yes. Wait a minute." There was quite a deal of grunting and puffing.

"Are you trying to pull the lever?" he asked.

"Of course, I am, you dingbat," grunted Hypotenuse. "It's just that the lever is very big, isn't it?"

There was a thump and a clunk and the door swung open. Hypotenuse was on the floor on her back next to a big lever.

"No time for lying around," said Pollig. "We've got to rescue Twelve."

They raced on but, as they got to a corner, skidded to a less suspicious walk. Two burly orcs in spikey armour were on guard in front of a big door with the words Treasure Vault above it in big fancy letters.

"Oi, goblin," said one of them. "Who are you and what's that?" The orc waved her nasty spikey weapon at Hypotenuse.

Pollig thought fast (although he could think fast, he could rarely think deep, which might be one reason why he frequently found himself in trouble).

"Prisoner transfer," he lied smartly. "From, er, cell block one-one-three-eight."

"What?" said Hypotenuse.

Pollig scooped her up in his arms.

"We weren't told," said the orc.

"Yes, she's a very dangerous prisoner," said Pollig. "Secret transfer."

"And what's that for?" said the other orc, pointing at Pollig's wobbly puffblower.

"In case she tries to escape," said Pollig. He moved on swiftly before they could think to question him again.

"That door..." said Hypotenuse once they were safely around the next corner. "It said 'treasure

vault'."

"I know," said Pollig.

"Treasure vault!"

"I know."

"Treasure!!" The tiny dragon's eyes were gleaming. "You said you'd help me find some treasure."

"Not Lord Dread's treasure! Only a fool would try to steal that. We'll find you some other treasure, after we've rescued Twelve."

There were unhappy noises coming from a nearby door. Pollig crept over and peered in. He could see Twelve inside on a chair, with two Spooks looming over him.

"No! No! Stop!" Twelve was wailing in horror.

"Tell us ha-what we need to know, sir, and the torture ha-will stop."

"Please! No!" Twelve cried.

"What's going on?" whispered Hypotenuse, horrified and fascinated in equal measure. "Let me see. No, I don't want to see. Tell me what's happening. No, don't tell me."

Pollig watched the torture, more surprised than anything. While Twelve sat in the high chair, the Spook waved a bowl of yellow slop under his nose while the other offered him a spoon dripping with the stuff.

"I shan't eat it! I shan't!" cried Twelve.

"Yellow slops. Twelve's secret weakness, his one fear," whispered Pollig. "I quite like the stuff actually. Bit vinegary I suppose, but it's really nice on toast."

"They're giving him dinner?" said Hypotenuse.

"Twelve loathes yellow slop," said Pollig. "Right. Time to do some rescuing. First, we'll distract them with the stinkfrond."

Pollig took some of the stinkfrond and crushed it in his hand. He held his hand out and, with a quick puff, blew it into the room.

"Oh, ha-what is that noxious odour?" the first spook said.

"Not me," said Twelve.

"Are those orc guards ha-washing their underwear again?" said the second Spook.

"It's disgusting ha-whatever it is!" said the first Spook. "Fresh air is called for!"

The Spook lunged forward and pushed the room door open. Pollig was not expecting this and stumbled backwards. He fell over Hypotenuse, who was at his feet trying to hear what was going on.

Pollig felt as if he was falling in slow motion. His eyes were drawn to the puffblower as he sailed backwards and down onto his bottom. For a moment, he thought he was going to keep it safe, as his arm was at its full extent with the puffblower in the air. Unfortunately, he kept rolling back. He completed a backwards roly-poly (which at any other time he would have been excited about) but now he didn't even know which way was up, and he'd lost track of where the puffblower was.

POOF!

The puffblower exploded.

Pollig skidded backwards across the floor, and Hypotenuse slammed into his legs. Pollig, Hypotenuse, the two Spooks and Twelve were all covered in the revolting sticky spores. It was like gritty treacle, and Pollig found it hard to even blink his eyes, as his eyelids were glued to his head.

"Hey Comrade Pollig!" shouted Twelve from inside the room. He was crawling to his feet, but he seemed to have an important question. "Why do you smell of orc's underwear?"

12

Pollig stumbled to his feet, staggered back and walked straight into one of the many wanted posters stuck to the walls.

"Bleargh!" he spat, trying to get the sticky gunk off him. Having a poster stuck to his face only made matters worse.

"So is this a rescue mission?" asked Twelve.

"Er, yes," he said, remembering himself. He grabbed Twelve in his now sticky hands and fled.

"Stop!" demanded a gunked-up Spook. "Running away from captivity is against the rules!"

Pollig ran as fast as he could but it wasn't easy to run when you were covered in puffblower gunk and had a wanted poster covering you from head to knees.

"He ha-went this way!" came a Spook yell.

The corridor Pollig had chosen came to a dead end. Behind him were the sounds of slapping feet chasing after him. "Biscuits!" he muttered frantically.

There was nowhere to hide. In utter desperation, he pressed himself flat against the wall and tried to make himself as thin as possible.

Two sticky Spooks came drifting along. They looked deeply unhappy but, then again, Spooks looked deeply unhappy most of the time. There was a pair of orc guards with them.

"I'm sure he came this way," said one of the orcs, looking round.

"Ha-wherever he is, we must find him," insisted a Spook.

They were so close, Pollig could hear the rasping breathing sounds of the angry Spooks and he could smell the orcs' breath. He froze and wished himself invisible.

Eventually, the Spooks and the orcs ran off to look for him elsewhere.

"I can't believe we got away with that," Pollig whispered in amazement.

Glued to Pollig's hand with fungus slime, Twelve looked up at Hypotenuse, who was similarly stuck to Pollig's shoulder.

"Greetings, Comrade Dragon. How long have you been stuck to my friend, Comrade Pollig?"

"Too long," said Hypotenuse, who was not enjoying the experience.

"I've only been doing it for a few minutes," said Twelve. "I'm not sure I like it much."

"Let's get out of here," said Pollig. "We can complain about how sticky we are later."

He peeled himself off the wall and crept back along the corridor, fearful of bumping into orcs or Spooks again. He stopped by a metal grille.

"A ventilation shaft! These lead up into the upper levels of the Fortress. We can sneak out of here."

Soon the grille cover was taken off and the three of them were inside, stickily climbing hand over hand up the square shaft and then, as it bent, along a distance. The metal tube creaked and echoed with their every movement.

"We're getting this shaft all dirty," noted Twelve as they shuffled along on sticky hands and knees.

"And guess whose job it is to clean it every week," muttered Pollig.

"And get rid of the spiders too," Twelve reminded him.

"Sp-spiders?" said Hypotenuse, stopping suddenly. She turned round on her tiny feet to face Pollig. "Are there spiders in this place?"

Pollig looked at the spiders in the corners of the shaft. He looked at Hypotenuse. He looked at the spiders again. He didn't want a startled spider-fearing dragon letting loose a fireball in this confined space. An explosion in here would be more than he could bear.

"Now, I don't want you to panic," said Pollig.

"Why would I panic?" said Hypotenuse.

"And I definitely don't want you to turn round."

"Why shouldn't I turn round?" said the dragon, beginning to do just that.

"No!" Pollig yelled and leapt to grab the tiny creature.

He grabbed hold of her, tumbled forward, and collided with a grille that was, unluckily, not as tightly fitted as Pollig would have liked. Pollig and Hypotenuse tumbled through and fell straight down, down onto a slipping and sliding pile of gold coins! Pollig looked around. They had dropped directly into Lord Dread's treasure vault!

The huge room was full of gold and silver, of treasures and rare gems. Everything Lord Dread had stolen in his ongoing rampage across the land was in this room! And here and there were the amazing (and occasionally successful) superweapons Lord Dread had used to steal the treasure.

"Gold!" hooted Hypotenuse in delight. "Gold! Gold! Gold!"

She danced around it in. She burrowed in it. She did high leaps and pirouettes on it.

"It's gold! And it's all mine!" she declared.

"Er, no, it's not," said Pollig. "And we need to get out of here before someone realises we've broken in."

At that moment, an alarm bell started ringing and red lights started flashing and a big voice said, "Alert! Alert! Thieves have broken into the treasure vault!"

"Oh, biscuits!" muttered Pollig.

Up high, there was a joyful cry and Twelve leapt from the ventilation shaft and onto a mountain of gold. He gave out a "Wheeeeee!"of excitement as he slid down.

"This is fun, Comrade Pollig," he said. "What's the plan then? What are we doing next?"

Pollig, gold stuck to his hands and Paddon Watt's face stuck to his own, stared around at the secure room they were trapped in.

"I have absolutely no idea," he said.

13

The big secure door to the treasure vault opened and the armies of Lord Dread poured in. Trolls with big swinging clubs. Dark wizards twirling balls of green fire. Cockalorum battalions singing their motivational battle chants ("Stab 'em, stab 'em. Stab 'em wiv the stabby thing."). Soldiers and generals and monsters of all description rushed in.

"Maybe we should hide," suggested Twelve.

"I don't have a better suggestion," said Pollig and so they ran off to hide.

"There he goes!" yelled a troll. "It's Paddon Watt! He looks just like his face on the poster!"

Pollig wanted to shout back that he wasn't Paddon Watt but what good would that have done?

They skidded round hill-sized piles of treasure and waded through shallow dips of coins. Pollig accidentally put his foot in a crown and stumbled for several seconds before he could dislodge it.

They couldn't see but could definitely hear Lord Dread's horde chasing after them through Lord Dread's hoard.

"What's this?" said Hypotenuse, staring up.

They had come to a wall along which were arranged a number of strange contraptions and devices. Some had giant cogs and massive pistons. Some were all glass chambers and strange tubes filled with liquid. Some fizzed with chemicals or wild electricity.

"These are all Lord Dread's old secret weapons. Every time he gets bored of one or it fails to work as expected, it gets brought down here," said Pollig.

"That's the Everwinter Sphere!" said Twelve, waving at a huge glass apparatus. "And there's the Bee-Bee Gun, capable of firing up to a hundred angry bees per minute!"

"No time for sight-seeing," said Pollig. "We're being chased, remember?"

"Oh, and the Gravimatrix!" said Twelve, pointing at a great big red On button. "Remember that? I didn't know which way I was going when that was switched on."

"I said—" But no one got the chance to hear what Pollig was going to say he'd said because, at that instant, a Spook popped up from the shadows and grabbed him.

"I have him," declared the Spook victoriously. "Enemy number one!"

"What?" squealed Pollig.

"Exactly," said the Spook.

"And his accomplice!" declared the other Spook snatching up Hypotenuse.

Hypotenuse did not react well to being snatched up by surprise. She made a high-pitched hoot of alarm. Pollig saw a lick of flame at the end of her nose.

"Uh-oh," he said and closed his eyes.

There was an almighty FOOM!

And abruptly there wasn't a Spook holding a tiny dragon anymore. The Spook was there with empty hands, a surprised look on its face and sooty scorch marks over every inch of it.

Hypotenuse had shot from its grasp, propelled by the dragon-sneeze explosion and into the nearest pile of treasure.

There was also now a massive hole in the wall. Outside, Pollig could see green fields and blue skies and the great big tyre tracks Fortress Dread was leaving in the landscape. Pollig had blown a hole right through the exterior wall of the Fortress!

The Spook holding Pollig gasped at the hole.

"Is this how you planned to escape?" it demanded.

"No," said Pollig who (it has been mentioned) was capable of thinking quickly but not as deeply as might be wise. "But this is!"

He slapped a hand on the huge On button of the Gravimatrix. The machine burbled and coughed, and sputtered into action.

The Gravimatrix, which had made the great big mess in Dr Darkbottom's laboratory and caused all manner of upset for people in the Fortress recently, worked by changing the direction of gravity. Down stopped being down and became sideways. Left became up and right became down.

At once, the wall of the vault had become the floor. The masses of treasure in the vault all started to slide backwards. Barrels of money rolled, diamonds tumbled and all manner of pretty jewellery flew through the air.

And out the hole.

The Spook who had only recently grabbed Hypotenuse got a big silver dish in the face, spilled through the hole and was gone. The Spook holding Pollig fell against the floor (which used to be the wall).

As precious metals flew by like gleaming hailstones, Pollig saw Twelve falling towards the hole. He reached out and snagged his friend and then, a moment later, caught hold of Hypotenuse too.

As treasure and trolls and orcs and wand-waving magic users rolled and flowed, Pollig and his friends lay pinned to the wall (now floor) beside the hole, held helpfully in place with sticky puffblower juices.

Lord Dread's accumulated wealth poured out of the hole and out into the blue sky.

"My treasure!" cried Hypotenuse.

"It's not your treasure!" Pollig shouted.

"A dragon has to have treasure, flip-flop!"

She wriggled out of his grip and as the very last of the gold fell through the hole, she ran to the edge and jumped through after it.

There was a whir and a clunk and the Gravimatrix switched off. Pollig looked round to see that Twelve had managed to crawl, sticky fist over stick fisty, like some climbing frog-thing to get to the off switch.

Down abruptly became down again. Pollig fell to the proper floor once more. Hundreds of orcs and trolls and wizardy-types also fell to the floor in an untidy mass.

"Ha-where has he gone?" said one Spook who had not fallen through the hole.

"Er," said Pollig, preparing to run again.

"You, goblin. Ha-where has that Paddon Watt character gone?"

Pollig patted his face. In the gravity-shifting silliness, the poster had been ripped from his face and had gone, along with the treasure out of the hole in the side of the Fortress.

Pollig pointed at the hole wordlessly.

"Escaped, has he? Thank you, young goblin," said the Spook and leapt out of the hole in pursuit of a dangerous criminal who had never existed.

Twelve unstuck himself from the Gravimatrix machine and hugged Pollig's leg. "Thank you, Comrade Pollig. Best rescue mission ever."

In the vast and now mostly empty treasure vault, the many minions of Lord Dread groaned and moaned as they tried to untangle themselves from one another.

"You know, someone's going to have to tidy this up," said Twelve.

"I've got a broom somewhere," said Pollig.

14

Far away, in the city of Alderbaron, it was market day. The sun was shining and the people of Alderbaron were happily about their business. They had a noble queen and shiny knights. They had efficient sewers and free-to-use public libraries. There was a lot for the people of Alderbaron to be happy about, and they were all starting to forget about that nasty Lord Dread who had tried to destroy their city with his anti-gravity ray.

One of the market traders happened to look up and see a long glistening cloud of gold in the sky. As she stared, others also looked up.

"What is that?" said one person.

"Is it rain?" said another.

"Is it gold?" said a third.

"It's raining gold!" someone yelled.

"Impossible!" yelled another voice.

"Wonderful!" cried a third.

"Blessed, blessed gold!" said a man, taking off his hat to catch the falling treasure as it rained down on the city.

"Hooray!" shouted the people of Alderbaron,

shortly followed by, "Ow! Ow! It's hitting me! It really hurts!"

The hat-owning man quickly put his hat back on to protect his head and ran for shelter, as did everyone else.

Many hours later, while the people of Alderbaron were hiding indoors and thinking of writing a sternly worded letter to their queen about the dangerous weather they'd just experienced, a voice could be heard in the streets.

"It's my treasure. My treasure! All mine! You hear me, you flip-flops?"

15

There was a lot of tidying up to be done in Fortress Dread. With all the chaos and damage and the large number of injured wizards, trolls and orcs (many who had hurt themselves on their own spikey armour), there seemed to be little that Pollig and his broom could do to fix it.

But eventually all was made right. Holes in walls and floors were patched. Spills were mopped up, and broken things were either mended or at least swept out of sight.

A pair of nesting glove-birds flapped overhead as Pollig and Twelve finished their chores and then they went to the gnome canteen for dinner. Pollig was squashed up at the far end, looming over the tiny table next to Twelve. Dinner was blue slop (which both of them liked) with a cup of tea on the side.

Soon, with the aches of a hard day's work in their bones, Pollig and Twelve retired to their beds. The gnomes had dormitory bedrooms, but the gnome beds were far too small for a goblin, even a goblin as small as Pollig. Also, officially, the beds

and the blankets and pillows were only for the use of gnome guild members so, instead, he slept in a hammock made from an old carpet hung between the ceiling pipes in the kitchen.

As he settled down to sleep, with the rumbling of the Fortress engines gently rattling the plates on the shelves, Pollig heard a scurrying scampering sound on the floor.

"If that's spiders," he said, "can you get rid of yourselves, please. I'm off duty."

The scurrying and scampering thing made a dismissive noise.

Pollig leaned over the edge of his hammock. In the shadows on the floor, the smallest (and largest) dragon he'd ever met looked back up at him.

"You came back," he said.

Hypotenuse opened her mouth and something heavy and shiny dropped onto the floor.

"Is that a gold coin?" said Pollig.

"It's my treasure hoard," she said.

"It's just one coin. I think you need more than one to have a hoard."

"Even the Queen of Dragons can only carry so much, dingbat," she said. "I'm sure the rest of it will be along in a bit."

"It really doesn't work like that," he said.

"Sure it does. It's like those things that, you know, stick together."

"Rice," said Pollig.

"I was going to say friends but, sure, whatever."

The tiny dragon walked round in a little circle and then laid down on her hoard under Pollig's hammock and went to sleep. Soon enough, to the sound of Hypotenuse's gurgling snores, Pollig went to sleep too.

THE END!!

Printed in Great Britain
by Amazon

60748537R00071